MW01235306

Chapter One

"Another boring day," Paige thought, staring at the television despite the fact that it wasn't turned on.

At nineteen, still living at home with her mother, she was finding herself at loose ends. Tired of the endless hassle of looking for a job, and never finding one, she knew she really should have worked harder in school to make good grades, instead of spending her time focused on her social life.

Getting a scholarship to college had been out of the question. Just passing the ACT test had been out of the question.

Paige collapsed onto the couch cushions, tossing the remote onto the nearby coffee table. The blank television screen gave back her blond haired, blue eyed reflection.

Moments later, Christina Banks walked through the door with a huge smile on her face.

"I've got good news," Christina told her daughter. "Your search for a job is over. The hospital is planning to hire two aides, and I've used my pull to get you an interview."

Twenty years before, Christina had first begun working at Bethany Hospital as a nurse. She was now head of the neo-natal unit.

Paige bounced up off of the couch and stared at her mother for several long moments as the words sank in.

"Seriously?" She finally asked, hands on her hips, attitude sticking out all over her. "Are you kidding? Wiping butts and emptying bed pans is not my idea of a job!"

Christina stared back at her daughter in silence, not in the least surprised at the reaction. It was what she had expected.

But she was silently wondering what she could possibly say that might help motivate the twenty year old to grow up.

"My job at the hospital has provided us with a good living for twenty years," she said at last, opting for a direct approach. "Stop being selfish and self-centered and at least, give this a try."

Paige wasn't prepared to give in, and her attitude was getting really spiky.

"First, Mom, you didn't ask me if I was interested in the job. You just told me to go apply. You decided, and I'm just supposed to follow your orders. And that's a whole different story."

Rolling her eyes, Paige slammed off to her room, unhappy with the feeling that her mother was still trying to run her life, despite the fact that she was legally of age. It was time for her mother to start showing her a little bit more respect.

Christina sighed. Although she had expected Paige's reaction, she knew it was time for her daughter to learn to accept some responsibility for her own life. Reality was that part of existence where big ideas and dreams had to be brought down to earth.

She kicked off her shoes, realizing her tired feet needed a soak, but putting it off. She had to get dinner, clean up the kitchen, vacuum the floor, put away the magazines Paige had left lying about, and then…

Then she could soak her tired feet.

Chapter Two

The next morning, Christina slid quietly into her daughter's room, gently touched her on the shoulder and said, "Your interview is at ten. Get up and start getting ready so you can be on time."

Still half asleep, Paige mumbled, "Okay Mom," and half tumbled, half crawled out of bed.

She would go, because she knew her Mom would give her a hassle if she didn't. She would have to at least show up.

No one would ever be able to prove that she had botched the interview on purpose!

Christina left for work, knowing in advance that Paige was going to blow the interview. She couldn't help but laugh at the futility of her own efforts.

Standing beneath the warm flow of water in the shower, Paige's mind was occupied with the upcoming interview, working out which method might be the most useful to employ to blow her chances of getting the job. Excessive make-up, tight clothes, not brushing her teeth, and last but not least, a bit more of that attitude she had been using on her mother the previous night!

When Paige reached the employment office at the hospital, the waiting room was full of applicants. She smiled, thinking, "No butts or bedpans for me! Someone here is bound to be more qualified than I am!"

Paige's name was called and she made her way into the office. She hadn't worn the tight dress or too much make-up, and she had brushed her teeth.

She figured attitude was all she really needed.

The head of human resources was explaining that this particular job was in the nursery on the midnight shift.

Eleven at night until seven in the morning.

Speechless, Paige was envisioning herself buried up to her kneecaps in crying babies, dirty diapers, and puke, while being perpetually sleep deprived. No way did she want this job!

"This is not at all what I was expecting," she told the woman, trying her attitude on for size. "I'm not comfortable handling newborns."

The woman didn't seem to have heard her. "Your job will encompass cleaning up in the nursery, running errands for the nurses, and helping with the babies. You start tonight at eleven o'clock. Report to the nurses' station thirty minutes early, there will be more forms for you to fill out, and a time sheet."

Feeling as if she had just somehow been railroaded into a job, Paige gave the woman her paperwork and left.

On the way to her car, she couldn't help thinking to herself, "This nightmare is just beginning, and I owe it all to my mom! Gee, thanks, Mom!"

The only thing Paige could do now was go home and have a pity party for herself and try to get a nap. It was going to be a long, long night!

By the time she arrived home, however, Paige had had some time to think. She wasn't thrilled with the job, but she did realize, belatedly, that her mother had only been trying to help. And at the very least, maybe this job would help alleviate some of the boredom she had been experiencing lately.

Even crying babies and dirty diapers might be better than sitting at home, staring at a blank television screen.

Chapter Three

Christina had supper going when Paige came in the kitchen and seated herself at the table.

"I'm not like you mom, but I'm going to give this job a chance," Paige said.

Christina smiled at her daughter and nodded. "Taking this job is a big challenge, and I'm proud of you. When your perfect job does comes along, this will look good on your resume."

After supper, Paige went to get ready for work. When she emerged an hour later, her mom wished her good luck, reminding her to be careful while driving to work. "The first night might be unnerving," she cautioned, hugging Paige before she headed out the door, "but it will get better, I promise."

A tall, slender blonde was waiting for Paige when she stepped out of the elevator onto the seventh floor of Bethany Hospital.

"My name is Joyce," the woman told her, "but everyone calls me Jay Jay. We will be working together every night. If you have any questions or issues just come to me."

"Thanks," Paige responded.

Jay Jay took Paige to the nurse's lounge, found her a locker, and produced a uniform for her to wear.

"Your mask, gloves and shoe coverings will be at the entrance to the nursery. Anytime you're in the nursery these items are required because it's a sterile environment."

When they reached the brightly lit nursery, the room was clean and warm. Every crib had shelving that held necessities for a baby, and Jay Jay showed Paige what needed to be cleaned and what needed to be replenished for every crib.

One corner of the nursery was closed off with a curtain. On the other side of the curtain were five rocking chairs, a bin of blankets, and a radio.

Jay Jay told Paige to dust mop the floor, replenish the bins, and take her fifteen minute break at one o'clock.

"It's probably not as bad as I'm making it out to be," Paige thought. "It's early yet and anything could happen."

Paige began to mop the floor. Since the cribs were on wheels, she moved them all allowing her to clean the whole area at one time, instead of mopping around each one.

"Chalk one up for me," Paige thought.

There were four babies in the nursery. One baby, born prematurely, was the size of a doll. Paige was very careful not to bump the incubator in which the baby was resting.

A small feather on the floor caught her eye, and Paige bent down to pick it up, thinking it must have come from a mattress. Then she realized there was no mattress.

She slipped it into her pocket and finished cleaning the area.

It was time for her break so she put the dust mop away and went to the nurses' lounge. The main area had two couches, four chairs and a television. In the back was a small kitchen with a table and chairs, a microwave, a fridge and a drink machine.

Paige got a cup of coffee and sat down on the couch. Jay Jay showed up moments later.

"Everything going okay?" She asked, sipping her coffee as she seated herself near Paige.

"It will be better at seven in the morning," Paige

replied dryly.

Jay Jay laughed. "Put your big girl panties on and make the best of it, my friend. Yes, the hours are lousy, but the pay isn't bad. And there are worse jobs you could have than this."

"You're right," Paige responded, wondering if her fake enthusiasm was showing through. In the back of her mind, she was still forming strategies to get herself out of this job.

"I found a feather on the floor while I was cleaning around the incubator, and I couldn't figure out where it came from," Paige remarked as their break ended and they both headed back to the nursery.

"Not the first time, believe it or not," Jay Jay nodded. "Feathers have been found in the nursery many times over the years. No one has discovered the source. Nothing in the nursery actually contains feathers."

As they reached the nursery, Paige could hear all of the babies crying.

"It's feeding time and this is when you help handle the babies. Come with me," Jay Jay said.

After preparing the bottles, Paige and Jay Jay each took two babies, one in each arm. Pretty cool plan, Paige thought, as she settled herself in one of the rocking chairs.

Easier said than done, however. One baby was spitting up, and the other had a dirty diaper. The combination was enough to make her start to gag.

By lunch time, Paige was more than ready for a break.

She decided to spend the forty-five minutes exploring the rest of the seventh floor.

The floors were all a beige colored tile, shining like glass from repeated cleaning. The place was quiet, and only dimly lit during the night shift. At one end of the hall Paige discovered a set of bathrooms, with storage rooms and offices at the opposite end.

To the right was a small lobby with chairs and a television. To the left was a short hallway, at the end of which were two benches positioned before a softly lit wall.

As she got closer, Paige realized it was a wall of plaques, each plaque bearing a name and date on it. Above the plaques it read, "The Angel Wall."

These children must have died here, Paige thought.

The area was very quiet and peaceful, the wall visually beautiful, each plaque shining like gold.

As she turned to leave, Paige had a sudden eerie feeling, like a tingling across the surface of her skin, but she shrugged it off. Probably the same feeling most people had in this sad but beautiful place.

As she reached the main hall, a woman passed her without speaking. Glancing back, Paige saw the woman seat herself on one of the benches in front of the Angel Wall.

Paige paused near the lounge to wait for Jay Jay. As they returned to the nursery, a doctor was complaining at the nurses' desk.

Jay Jay explained that this particular doctor was consistent, focused and most times inflexible.

"Pinhead," Jay Jay muttered. "He'll just have to get over it!"

Paige smirked, "You must not like him very much!"

Jay Jay smirked back, "Neither will you!"

Paige quickly realized that she was in capable hands with Jay Jay.

"A piece of advice, Your Barbie doll life has ended. Deal with it and learn to roll with the flow." Jay Jay remarked.

It was feeding time again, but it was time for one of the other nurses to help. Paige spent her time restocking the bins for the next shift about to come on.

Before she knew it her shift was almost over. She had made it through the night and learned some things in the process.

Jay Jay tapped her on the shoulder and said, "Good job tonight. I enjoyed working with you. I hope to see you back tonight."

Chapter Four

When Paige walked out of the hospital, the morning sun was blindingly bright. That was something she hadn't seen since her school days.

Amazed that she had survived her first night on the job, she did a happy dance all the way to her car, singing, "Oh yes, I'm the one. I did it, I did it!"

As she was leaving the parking lot, she saw her mom, just arriving for work. Paige gave her a thumbs up sign, knowing her mother would be happy to learn that she had made it through the first night without any problems.

The house was empty and quiet when she got home, and she put on her pajamas and climbed into bed, snuggling down into the covers for a well-deserved rest.

The sound of a door closing woke her up. Then she heard her mom calling her name. Paige rolled over and looked at the clock. It was four o'clock.

She closed her eyes again, but very shortly thereafter, the smell of ham and eggs cooking got her out of bed and lured her into the kitchen.

"Mom, thanks for helping me get this job," she murmured begrudgingly, seating herself at the kitchen table. Amazed to hear herself thanking her mother for helping her get a job she had originally intended to botch. "I still don't care for the hours, but it is an interesting place to work."

"I heard good things about your first night," Christina nodded, equally amazed to hear her daughter thanking her, without the usual bit of bad attitude. "Just do your best, sweetheart. When something better comes along and you need to quit, I'll understand."

Paige showered and dressed. Dinner was ready by

the time she got back to the kitchen.

"What did you like most about your first night at work?" Christina asked around a forkful of food.

Paige couldn't help but smile. "The babies, of course! How could anyone not like babies?"

They continued to chat as they ate, and Paige surprised herself by not developing an attitude even once during dinner.

She surprised her mother as well.

The drive to Bethany Hospital was peaceful, with very little traffic. Stars lit up the sky like a scattering of diamonds across black velvet, and the silver sphere of the full moon turned the night into magic.

How many times in my life have I missed this beautiful sight?

As she pulled into the parking lot, she noticed two police cars and an ambulance near the emergency room entrance.

Not an uncommon sight at a hospital.

Police officers were also on the seventh floor.

Standing at the nurses' station, Jay Jay waved Paige over, then pulled her aside.

"A child was found in a dumpster, wrapped in a dirty towel, left to die," Jay Jay whispered. "She is barely five hours old, but she's still clinging to life. There will be people in and out of here all night, so stay alert. It's going to be chaotic!"

Paige started her shift by dust mopping the floor. There were only two babies in the nursery tonight. The child found in the dumpster was in an incubator, in a critical care area.

Paige felt as if her heart was breaking, unable to think of anything except the unloved child who had been left to die. The unloved child who probably wasn't going to survive the night.

Chapter Five

Jay Jay and another nurse were feeding the two babies when the baby in the incubator went into crisis and all hell broke loose. Alarms sounded as the doctors tried to save her.

Death hovered in the corner of the room, waiting.

Completely unnerved, Paige left the nursery area and stood outside the viewing window.

An hour later, the child was dead.

An undercurrent of sadness drifted through the nursery. This child had died alone, with no one to love her, to kiss her, or to say good-bye.

What a horrible night.

As the child's body was being taken to the morgue, Paige went back into the nursery to clean up the area.

Jay Jay gave Paige a wise, compassionate look and shrugged. "This is part of what we do and who we are. In a case like this, we try to help, when and where we can. So many times we search for a deeper understanding of why these things happen, but rarely does an answer come. Just try to do your job. Don't let your mind dwell on this."

Paige nodded, not trusting herself to respond.

Underneath the incubator she found another small, white feather.

"Strange," she thought, as she once again pocketed her find.

Break time arrived and Paige was more than ready for it. Cradling her coffee cup, she deposited herself on the couch, staring out the small window at the starry night.

Surprisingly, she found herself thinking of her own mother, grateful that her mom had loved her enough to give her life. She bowed her head, silently thanking God for giving her such a wonderful mother, silently asking Him to watch over the child who had recently arrived in Heaven.

"Time to get back to work," Jay Jay's voice was quiet.

Five people were standing near the nurses' station as they returned, two of them police officers. The young girl, in handcuffs, was surrounded by her parents, both of whom looked as if they had just been handed their own death sentences.

No doubt there would be criminal consequences. The girl had made her own life a living hell, destroying her parents' lives as well.

Jay Jay informed the family and police that the child had died. She called for the doctor and took the family to the waiting room.

Paige walked in the nursery and continued to clean up and re-stock the bins. A few minutes later, a newborn was brought to the nursery. Paige watched as they cleaned him up, checked him out, and then wrapped him in a warm blanket.

When she turned around, the viewing window was full of people waiting to see the new baby. Tears swelled in her eyes as she thought, "that is exactly how it is supposed to be."

When lunch time arrived, Paige headed down to the ground floor and walked outside, wanting to be alone. She looked up toward the sky, still thinking of that tiny life, so recently extinguished, and of her own life, and the love of her own mother. Tonight's tragedy had changed and humbled her.

The rest of the night was quiet, except for the normal routine of caring for the babies.

"Time to go," Jay Jay said finally.

Paige and Jay Jay walked out together. They were both off for the next two nights, giving them a chance to rest, and to try to put this tragedy behind them.

When Paige got in her car, she just sat there lost in thought. She was startled by a knock on her window.

It was her mom.

"Is something wrong?" Christina asked.

Paige wiped away a single tear, threatening in the corner of her eye.

"It's been a terrible night, Mom. They brought in a child that was found in a dumpster, but the child died," Paige replied.

Christina's voice was sympathetic. "Life and death darken these doors every day, sweetheart. We do the best that we can, but sometimes, it's just not enough. Go on home and get some rest. It'll help."

Paige didn't remember ever having felt heartbreak like this in her life, and found herself overwhelmed that she could feel such a strong emotion for a child she had never known.

Not knowing why this tragedy had to have happened, simply made it unbearable.

Chapter Six

Paige lay across her bed, weeping from a mixture of sadness and guilt. Thoughts and memories of her own childhood were so happy that she couldn't help but feel a sense of guilt when she thought of the little girl who never had a chance.

Last night's tragedy had transformed her life and today, she was a different person. No more pity parties, no more thinking only of herself.

She knew her life had been blessed, and it was time she stared acting like it.

Paige took two aspirin for a pounding headache, hoping it would subside enough for her to sleep.

Two hours later, she was still awake.

She decided to surprise her mom by cleaning the house, something she rarely did.   Now, she was doing it just to please her Mom.

She was surprised how good that made her feel.

When Christina walked through the front door, she just stood there, inhaling that fresh cleaned house scent, caught completely off guard.

Even more importantly, something was smelling good from the kitchen.

Half laughing, half in disbelief, Christina yelled out, "Oh my goodness! What did I do to deserve this!"

Paige walked out of the kitchen, smiling, and hugged her mother's neck. "Just being my mom was enough."

Paige was no chef, but she made a pretty tasty pot of spaghetti. She had added a salad and some warm French bread, slathered with butter and garlic.

Christina couldn't seem to stop smiling.

When Paige got up the next morning, she found her mom in the kitchen. "Just in time for breakfast. How did you sleep?"

"I don't remember, so I must have slept pretty well," she responded, making herself a cup of coffee.

"What's on your agenda for today?" Christina asked.

Smiling, Paige replied, "Shopping and hanging out with my friends."

Christina nodded, thinking that a day out with friends would be a good remedy for the awful shift Paige had had two nights before.

Later, after her mom had left for work, Paige found herself staring at her own reflection in the mirror as she prepared to meet her friends. The little girl that used to stand there and brush her hair was now a woman, a working woman, beginning a new part of her life.

Paige smiled. "I'm looking too good for a trip to Wal-mart. It's a day at the mall for me!"

A full day of shopping with three girlfriends, two visits to the food court, and six hours of gossip, turned out to be as much excitement as she could stand for one day.

When she finally got home, her mom was already there. Paige couldn't wait to surprise her with a new blouse she had just bought for her mom. A small thank you that was way overdue.

Paige opened the door, paused and yelled, "I've got a happy for you mom! Where are you?"

"In the den," Christina replied. "This makes two days in a row that you've outdone yourself. Bring me my happy!"

Christina was delighted with the new blouse, and Paige couldn't stop smiling about her own considerate new attitude. She also brought home burgers and fries for supper, so there would be no cooking or clean-up tonight.

Christine got up out of her chair and put her arms around Paige. "You are amazing."

"Didn't you already know that?" Paige grinned.

When Paige got out of bed the next morning, her mom had already gone to work.

She realized that she was excited about her shift tonight. Two days off had given her a new perspective about many things. She was taking a new path.

"Amazing," Paige thought, "how just when we think we know it all, life teaches us a new lesson."

Christina called and told Paige that she would have to work overtime because one of the nurses had called in sick. She didn't know what time she would be home, but she didn't want her daughter to worry.

"Better get a nap and rest up. There are five babies in the nursery now and one more on the way," Christina told Paige.

"Thanks, Mom. See you when I see you," Paige replied.

When Paige left for work that night, her Mom still wasn't home. But when she got to the red light in front of the hospital, Paige saw her Mom right across the intersection from her. They tooted horns as they passed one another.

When Paige got to the seventh floor, she could hear babies crying. A sure sign that this night would be busy, very quickly. Paige saw Jay Jay and two other nurses through the window. She got ready and hurried in to help.

The diaper bin was full and stinky, so Paige took care of that first. Then she put clean pads and blankets in the cribs. She was getting a understanding of how important cleanliness was in the nursery.

Jay Jay got her attention, and gave her a wave to come join her for a break. Paige told her friend about her week-end, detailing each of the things she had done for her mom. It was apparent that she was proud of herself.

"A sign of maturity," Jay Jay remarked. "When you think of someone other than yourself it's a good feeling, and hopefully, something you will do more of."

They got some coffee, and Jay Jay surprised Paige with some donuts. Paige laughed and thought to herself, "Surely you are not going to share with anyone else but me. I could eat them all!"

After their break, Paige helped with the babies, changing diapers and putting clean sleepers on the babies. She was nervous about handling one particular baby because it was so small, but somehow, she managed.

Lunchtime came, and Paige decided to visit the Angel Wall. As she got to the end of the hallway, the lady she had seen the previous week was coming toward her. As she passed, the woman spoke.

"Good evening," she said. "You've grown into such a lovely young lady. I've known your mother since the day you were born."

"Thank you," Paige replied.

Paige asked the lady her name, but she continued on without answering.

"Maybe someone who used to work with my mom."

When Paige reached the Angel Wall, she sat down on one of the benches and gazed at the plaques.

She had a strange feeling. For a moment, just a moment, she thought she saw an image taking shape before her.

She closed her eyes and took a deep breath, thinking

that she was just sleepy. Maybe someone was playing a joke on her. Suddenly, she felt a soft breeze around her.

"Nobody will ever believe this. I'm out of here!" she said.

All the way back to the nursery she mumbled the word, "unbelievable!"

Jay Jay took one look at Paige and said, "What's wrong? You look like you saw a ghost or something."

Paige replied, "I actually think I might have. At the Angel Wall."

"A dimly lit hallway tends to set the mood for a ghostly happening. There have been many stories about things like that at the Angel Wall. I believe something watches over that very special place."

"Tonight has been an interesting night," Paige thought. "First I meet a lady who knows me, but she won't tell me her name. Then something really unexplainable happens at the Angel Wall. If I'm being set up. I will beat them at their own game. I'll go along with this, but in the end I'll have the last laugh!"

Over the course of the next two weeks, Paige got better at her job and began to enjoy it. Especially working with Jay Jay.

She had become intrigued with the Angel Wall, going there every night on her lunch break. Every time she got to the end of the hallway, she tip-toed around the corner, hoping to catch someone off guard, determined that the joke wouldn't be on her. Tenacity had its rewards!

But she never caught anyone.

At the end of her shift, she tidied up her area, took a last look around and prepared to go home.

Chapter Seven

Before Paige could reach the elevator, she heard Jay Jay calling her name. "Paige, don't leave, don't leave, your mother has been in a car accident. She's in the emergency room!"

"Oh God, Oh God," Paige screamed. "Take me to her!"

Jay Jay took her by the hand and said, "Take a deep breath and try to stay calm. We'll be there in a minute. I don't know any details, I just got the call."

When the elevator door opened, Paige ran to the nurses' station. "Where is my mother? What room is she in?"

"She has been rushed to surgery," the nurse replied. "Try to relax. We don't know anything yet."

Jay Jay led Paige to the waiting room. Paige stopped at the door and looked at Jay Jay. "I'm scared."

"Of course you are," Jay Jay replied, stroking her friend's hair to calm her. "Don't worry, I'll be right here with you. We will wait this out together."

The two of them sat in silence.

Paige sat in the waiting room with her knees pulled up to her chest, and her head bent down. With tears running down her face, she prayed. She had no choice but to wait this out.

A police officer came to the waiting room to talk to Paige. He came from the scene of the car accident to offer any information that he could.

He sat down beside Paige and said, "Let me tell you what I know, and maybe you can answer some questions for me. A man ran a red light this morning and hit your mom's car head on. When we got there, the man in the other car was too drunk to get out of his car. Your mom was pinned in her car, and she was unconscious.

"The firemen cut your mother out of her car. She was immediately brought here. The driver of the other car is in jail."

After a long silence, Paige spoke. "A drunk driver did this to my mom. Unbelievable! She is fighting for her life, and he is sobering up in jail."

Paige's anxiety for her mother was almost crippling.

The doctor came to the door and asked Paige and Jay Jay to join him out in the hall.

The surgeon said, "Christina's internal injuries are massive. She is stable for the moment, but it doesn't look good. We are taking her to Intensive Care. You need to go to the waiting room there. I will let you see her as soon as I can."

Paige fell to her knees and wept, uncontrollably. Jay Jay knelt beside her and said, "We need to go! Maybe you can see her when we get there."

Paige whispered, "What would I do without you? I have no one else."

Jay Jay replied, "So many people here know and love your mother. You won't be alone. Your faith is being tested, but don't let it go. You've just got to keep trusting that God's with her and you, too."

A nurse came to the waiting room and told Paige that she would be able to see her mother for ten minutes. Jay Jay promised to be there when Paige returned.

"It's the next room on the right," the nurse whispered in a sympathetic voice. "She is sedated, but it's still a good idea to talk to her and let her know that you are with her."

Paige pulled the curtain back and felt her strength

draining away from her as she looked at her mother's bruised and swollen face. Blood plasma was flowing into Christina's veins through an IV, she was hooked to six different machines, and there was a breathing tube down her throat.

"My God in Heaven! How can she survive this?" Paige whispered. "Have mercy, Lord God, have mercy."

She stood there staring down at her mother, frozen in time, as the various machines created a cacophony of beeps and chirps around her. Paige walked to the bedside, put her hand on her mother's arm, and leaned down close to whisper in a choked voice, "I love you, Mom. You had the courage to give me a fighting chance at life, now I need you to fight for your life. I don't have a life without you."

The response she had hoped for did not come, and when the nurse signaled her, Paige knew it was time to return to the waiting room. As she padded back through the silent hallway, her exhaustion began to catch up with her. Jay Jay could see it around her eyes when she came back into the waiting room.

"Come sit down," Jay Jay instructed, pulling her friend to one of the comfortable couches. "How is she?"

Paige shook her head, struggling to hold in the panic that was surging just below the surface of her composure. "It looks bad! I talked to her, but she didn't move or open her eyes, and I doubt she even knew that I was there. There isn't much I can do for now but wait and pray."

Jay Jay nodded. "I've got to head home for a little while, but I'll be back as soon as I can. There is a room on the seventh floor, for anyone that needs to stay overnight. It's there for you if you need it. I know it's difficult, but try to stay positive, Paige."

Paige watched Jay Jay leave, then glanced across at

the clock on the wall. "Two hours, and then I can see her again. Maybe next time she will be awake."

For the first time in many years, she longed to be surrounded by family members, to have a shoulder to cry on, a hand to hold, a companion who felt and understood the depths of her own fears.

Chapter Eight

Half an hour later, one of the nurses brought Paige a pillow and a blanket, and she stretched out in one of the recliners to try to rest for a few minutes. Despite her fears, her body was past going, her spirit sagging, and sleep overtook her before she even realized it.

When she awoke, one of the other nurses had brought her a lunch tray. She gobbled the food, realizing that she was only moments away from another opportunity to see her mother. Both the food and the rest strengthened her, and when the nurse poked her head in the door a few moments later, Paige was already standing, ready to go.

Paige hurried to the door so fast that she almost fell. She didn't even bother to put her shoes on.

As she pulled the curtain back, tears began running down her face when she saw that her mother's eyes were open.

"I love you," Paige whispered through a tremulous smile. "Welcome back."

Christina managed the barest hint of a smile, and whispered back, "I love you too!"

She didn't get to stay long. Christina's strength seemed to ebb away quickly, and the nurse quickly popped her head back in. "We don't want to tire her."

Paige nodded and tiptoed away. Jay Jay was in the waiting room, and Paige shared the wonderful news that her mom was awake.

"Hallelujah!" Jay Jay smiled. "Maybe the worst is over."

Jay Jay convinced Paige to go outside and get some fresh air, knowing her friend had been closed up inside of the hospital for far too long. As they walked outside, the sun was beginning to set, lighting up the western horizon with orange-red flames of color. How Paige wished her mom could see it. Maybe before long they would watch a sunset together.

Later, Paige decided to go up to the seventh floor and take advantage of the extra bed. Almost to the point of collapsing, she hesitated as she reached for the doorknob, then turned slowly instead and walked down to the Angel Wall. She sat down on the bench, and covered her face with her hands as the tears began to flow.

"Oh God, if there is an angel watching over this place, my mom needs one, too!" She whispered.

Paige searched the depths of her soul for answers. If there was one thing she could change, it would be the time that she didn't spend with her mother.

"This is me at my lowest." Paige thought. "What happens next? I just need to get through tonight. Tomorrow will bring issues of it's on."

A constant wave of memories filled her mind. Reliving them, to her, was a way of holding on.

Chapter Nine

She was awakened later when someone opened the door of the room.

"It's five thirty," Jay Jay whispered, "and visitation is in thirty minutes. Better get up."

Paige sat up in bed realizing that her mom had made it through the night. She got up, put her shoes on, washed her face and went to the waiting room.

When she got to her mother's room, she was shocked! Her mother was awake and the breathing tube was out.

"Oh, Mom, I've been so scared! How are you feeling? Do you remember what happened? Are you in pain? I've got a million questions, but I guess now is probably not the time."

Christina smiled, and held out her hand toward Paige. Paige held her mother's hand to her face, overwhelmed by her own emotions as the tears spilled down her cheeks, but joy filled her heart.

She looked up toward the ceiling, as if to by-pass it a million miles, and with a whisper said, "Thank you, God."

Christina attempted to speak. She said, "Go home. I'm okay now."

Paige started to respond, but her mother shook her head, no.

Finally Paige responded, "Okay, but I'll be back."

Paige did the happy dance all the way to the waiting room. When she sat down, the smile on her face said it all!

Jay Jay came in the waiting room for an update. The look on Paige's face told her the news had to be good. A smile from ear to ear and no tears. Yep, gotta be good!

"I believe Mom's on the road to recovery. She's awake, and she spoke to me," Paige said.

Jay Jay responded with a smile and said, "If all goes well for the next few days, I'll see you at work, soon."

"Consider it a date!" Paige replied.

Paige asked Jay Jay to spread the good news. She was going home for a while, but would be back later that afternoon.

Around lunchtime the doctor went in to see Christina. The swelling around her brain was getting worse, and he needed to do some scans.

Christina whispered, "You must not tell Paige any bad news. Discuss it with me first."

The doctor agreed, and they took her to Radiology.

The scans took longer than expected because they had to move her with extreme caution. Any unnecessary movement could affect her internal injuries, and the bleeding could start again, and she might not survive surgery.

Paige was in the waiting room for her afternoon visit, exited to see her mom, unaware of anything that was going on. All day she anticipated that her mom was getting better and would be going home soon.

Paige closed her eyes and whispered, "My mom is the best part of my life. Don't take this precious gift that you gave me. I am so thankful and from now on will always be."

Christina was sleeping when Paige walked in the room. She stood beside the bed, and her mother opened her eyes.

"How are you doing?" Christina murmured.

Paige answered, "Me? I'm much better now. I'll be great the day that you can go home. Close your eyes and rest, and I'll see you in the morning. I love you."

Paige went to the hospital cafeteria, got her a plate, and took it up to the nurses' lounge on the seventh floor. While she ate she shared the good news about her mom's progress.

It was almost time for Jay Jay to be at work, and she wanted to tell her about her mom, but until she got there, Paige decided to go to the Angel Wall and have some quiet time.

When she got to the end of the hallway, she saw the mysterious lady she had encountered before, the one who said she knew her. Hesitating, not wanting to impose on her time, Paige turned to leave.

"Join me, it's alright."

Paige responded, "My mom was in a car accident, and she's downstairs in ICU. I like to come here because it's a quiet, humbling place to think."

"I've been coming here for many years. I lost my daughter the day she was born. My decisions have haunted me, but God has shown me mercy," the lady said with great emotion.

"I'm so sorry," Paige said. "Is her name on the wall?"

"No," the lady replied. "Always in my heart and on my mind. I hope your mother gets better."

Before Paige could say another word. The lady got up and walked away.

Paige went to the nurses' station to update Jay Jay, and to tell her about the lady at the Angel Wall.

Jay Jay commented, "Great news about your mom! We have seen that lady many times over the years, but she doesn't work here. She is always by herself and never speaks. Don't try to figure that one out!"

Paige asked Jay Jay to give her a wake-up call at five thirty. She was going to bed hoping to catch up on some sleep. When Paige said her prayers, she prayed for something good, or something better the next morning.

Chapter Ten

Jay Jay went to wake Paige up, and found her sitting up in the bed. Paige turned her face toward Jay Jay and said, "I feel like I'm in an emotional trench. I don't like being here, but I don't know how to get out!"

"No one can tell what the future holds. Just try to be strong," Jay Jay said with compassion.

"What are my strengths?" Paige asked. "I know my weaknesses, but I don't know the limits of either one."

Jay Jay told her to come get a cup of coffee, and pull herself together before visiting her mom. "She's made it through another night. Be thankful and put a smile on your face."

"Thanks, Jay Jay. I couldn't get through this without you. Your help means more than you will ever know," Paige replied.

Christina was awake and propped up in the bed when Paige came in the room. One of her eyes was swollen shut. Although that concerned Paige, she didn't address it.

"Morning mom," Paige said. "How are you feeling this morning?"

Christina replied, "I have a terrible headache, but I'm hungry."

Their conversation was interrupted when the doctor came in the room. He needed to run a brain scan because the swelling around her brain wasn't subsiding and that concerned him.

Silence fell in the room.

"What are you saying?" Paige asked, following him out the door.

The doctor glanced back at her. "I'm sorry, Paige.

Your mother didn't want you to worry, and as her friend, I promised not to mention her problems in front of you. But it goes against hospital policy, and against my conscience."

"Don't let her die!" Paige pleaded.

"I wish it was up to me," he told her.

Paige went back to her mother's room, realizing that, with each passing moment, death was overtaking her mother's body.

A nurse sent Paige back to the waiting room as attendants came to take her mom for the scan. Paige moved to one side of the room, until they got her mother out, then she knelt down and prayed.

"Oh God," she cried. "What do I do now? I selfishly beg you to save the only person I've truly loved."

Something was very wrong, and Paige could feel it. She went back to the waiting room and tried to be as positive as she could.

"Part of me says it will be okay, but the other part isn't so sure," Paige said.

She counted the minutes until the next visit. When she got to her mother's room, the doctor was there, and her mom was awake.

The doctor took Paige aside and whispered, "She's dying, Paige, I'm sorry. There's nothing we can do but keep her comfortable. Before long she will go into a coma. She's already been told."

Paige moved back into the room, moving to her mother's side as Christina held out her hand.

"You've been my greatest gift," Christina smiled, "and I have no regrets. I have always loved you."

Barely able to get the words out, Paige replied, "You are my life, and the love I feel for you is endless."

Paige watched as her mother's eyes went dark and she took her last breath. Paige lay across her mother's chest, weeping like a lost child.

Within seconds every alarm in the room was going off! The doctor and nurses came running in the room, but she was gone.

Paige kissed her mother's forehead. One by one the nurses left the room, and the doctor said, "We have a hospital representative here to help you if you need one."

"Yes sir, I do." Paige replied. When the doctor left the room, Paige knelt at her mother's bedside and prayed. When she got up, she kissed her mother's face one last time.

Chapter Eleven

"I can't believe she's dead!" Paige whispered, choking on the words. Her tear streaked face was filled with anguish and disbelief. The necessary paperwork had been filled out, and Paige was sitting in her car. She banged on the steering wheel and screamed, flooded with emotions that were out of her control.

After a few minutes, she was finally able to compose herself and drive home.

She opened the front door of the now quiet house, suddenly shrouded in loneliness. All she could feel was a sense of disbelief.

"I'm afraid," Paige thought. "Where do I begin? Mom always handled everything. I've never even paid a bill!"

Within minutes, Paige was bombarded with phone calls. Co-workers and friends offering their support and sympathy.

Paige finally got a shower and tried to lie down, exhausted. When she lay across her bed, she let out a breath and looked around the room. In the back of her mind, her mother's death had consumed her.

It was just past sunset when she woke up. Everything seemed so unreal. The mother she so desperately needed and loved was gone.

Now in a silent house, Paige played her memories over and over in her mind. She began to sob, wiping the tears from her face. Finally facing the truth, she felt a sadness beyond tears.

She went to her mother's room, opened the door and stood there. Her feelings and mental pictures were overwhelming. She needed to look for insurance papers, or maybe a will.

Paige started in the closet. She found a large cardboard box, and a small metal box with the key taped on the top.

When she opened the flaps of the cardboard box, its contents were mainly memorabilia of Paige's childhood. Something to enjoy when her heart wasn't filled with grief. She put it aside.

She got the metal box and set it in her lap. It was packed with papers. She began the process of going through them one at a time.

The first envelope was her mother's life insurance policy. Paige stared at it in disbelief. It was for one hundred thousand dollars, and she was the beneficiary.

The next envelope contained the mortgage papers. The house was paid for and left to Paige. She felt that she found what was needed for now, and she could go through the rest of it later.

Her mom's death tore a place in her heart so devastatingly deep that it might never heal. She found it hard to focus on anything. The one constant was the silence in the house.

"I can't do this," Paige thought, "I can't, I won't." she began to cry. Her mom's death had eaten away at her life, leaving no room for anything else.

Anger and pain poured from her soul. Her true feelings were coming out, and her sense of loss had everything out of balance.

Paige looked at the clock, realizing that she had to be at the funeral home in an hour. She had the paperwork. Now she needed to pick the clothes and accessories for the funeral. She wanted her mom to look beautiful.

Paige looked at every outfit, hanger by hanger,

remembering how it looked on her mom. Blue was her favorite color, so blue it would be.

The jewelry would be a simple choice. Her mother didn't believe in buying a lot of things simply to have them. She was very frugal with her money.

She put her mother's clothes and life insurance policy in a small suitcase, and took them to the funeral home. When she got there, a lady took the suitcase, and told Paige that her mother would be ready for viewing in two hours.

"Make her as beautiful as you can." Paige asked.

"I'll do my best." she replied. "If you haven't chosen a pall for the casket, you might want to do that now. The shop next door has beautiful flowers."

Paige walked next door and the smell of fresh flowers was incredible! So many colors and varieties. "Mom always loved Yellow Roses. She'll have them now."

The lady stepped from around the counter, put her arms around Paige and just held her.

"It's okay to grieve." The lady remarked. "Just pray for the day when all you can remember are the good things."

Barely able to speak, Paige managed to thank her. She walked outside, took a deep breath and set down on a bench. When she composed herself, she walked back to the funeral home and went in. The lady told her everything was ready for her.

Before she could take a breath, Jay Jay was standing beside her. But Paige had reached her breaking point and fell to her knees.

Jay Jay knelt on the floor beside her. "This is not an easy thing to do. I will help you. Take my hand, and we'll do this together."

They got up from the floor and walked through the doors of the chapel. Paige stopped.

"I need a minute, I need a minute!" she cried.

"Take your time," Jay Jay said. "It's just you and me."

Paige reached for Jay Jay's hand, and they walked toward the casket. She could see her mother. She knew the next few steps would put them face to face.

Although there was still some visible swelling, the beautician had done an excellent job, and Christina looked as if she was sleeping.

The visitation was tomorrow at ten and the funeral was at eleven. There was an old cemetery on the outskirts of town where Christina would be buried. Paige had been there many times. Mostly as a child on Halloween night.

It was a beautiful place, surrounded by towering oak trees, lush green grass and fresh flowers at the graves. Most impressive were the old marble headstones, some dating back to the seventeenth century.

Jay Jay told Paige to go home and rest up for tomorrow. Everything was perfect for the funeral, but she needed to prepare for the deepest heartbreak imaginable tomorrow.

"See you tomorrow, then?" Paige asked.

"Without a doubt, just for you," Jay Jay replied.

Paige was exhausted. She needed a shower and some sleep.

"It still hurts," Paige thought, "knowing I'll never see my mom again."

Paige walked in the house, and her mind was flooded with memories. She walked room to room reliving moments spent there with her mother. Finally, she went to bed.

The next morning, it was almost seven when she woke up. The only thought on her mind was seeing her mom one last time. She fixed herself something to eat, got dressed and left for the funeral home at nine o'clock.

In the chapel co-workers had already gathered. Their kindness touched her heart and moved her to tears. The closer she got to the casket, the more she silently prayed for strength. Her mother looked at peace.

She stood there as if she was frozen in time. "I'll never look upon your face again." she whispered. Then she felt an arm around her shoulder. It was Jay Jay.

"Take it all in," Jay Jay whispered. "Let yourself grieve because this is your last good-bye."

Paige was trembling. She reached and touched her mother's hand. When she pulled her hand back, she pressed it to her lips, a final kiss, and placed it on her mother's face.

The service started and the casket was closed. Beautiful floral wreaths surrounded the casket, and the sound system played *Amazing Grace.*

Paige wept to the point that she could hardly catch her breath. The service was over, and the last leg of her journey was to the cemetery.

When the graveside service was over, Paige stood beside the casket, completely shattered. She found little comfort in anyone's words. Nothing could lessen the pain of burying her mother.

She knelt on the ground beside the casket, kissed it and whispered, "I have loved you all my life, as I know you have loved me."

Jay Jay helped her up and said, "Go home now."

Paige hugged her neck and replied, "Thank you, for

everything you've done for us. You truly are inspiring!"

Paige went home. It was hard for her to picture home, without her mom. She sat down and tried to sort things out in her mind, but found out it was more than she could do right now.

She walked through the house and memories of time spent there with her mom flooded her mind. Remembering made her realize how blessed she had been. Her mother took care of business and protected her to the end. She left nothing undone and gave it all. Now it was up to Paige.

Time will heal the sadness. One day, joy would sneak back into her memories and life would start anew. Sadness would only be a small part of an incredible life.

"Hardships have been minimal in my life," Paige remembered. "My mother made sure that they would stay that way in my future."

Paige had no intention of letting her mother, or herself, down. She would deal with her grief as time would allow, and become the woman her mother would've been proud of.

She said her prayers and went to bed. Tomorrow was a new day. Getting a grip on her life and moving forward was her goal.

Chapter Twelve

The next morning she woke up with a new perspective. To grow up, and become responsible with all her mom had left her.

She decided to start by going through the rest of her mom's papers. She went to her mom's room, got the metal box and took it to the kitchen table.

The key that was taped to the top of the box didn't match the lock. What did it go to, she wondered. Maybe a safety deposit box. She removed it and set it aside.

Most of the papers were relevant to their medical insurance. There were two death certificates, one for Christina's mother and one for her father. Both of her parents had been killed in a train accident when Christina was nineteen years old.

Paige thought, "How ironic that Mom lost both her parents when she was young, too. She must have felt then, what I feel now."

The rest of the papers were Paige's report cards, papers relevant to Christina's employment, and her nursing certificates.

Paige put everything back in the box, and put the box back in the closet. She was curious about the key, so she called the bank, and they confirmed that there was a safety deposit box.

She drove to the bank, wondering all the way. Inside the box, she found one big manila envelope. On the outside it read, "To Paige." It was dated three years before.

Paige didn't know what to expect. She took the envelope out, locked the box back up and took it home to view its contents.

Paige had just gotten home when there was a knock

at the door. It was Ms. Ellen with all of Mom's things from her office. There were three boxes and a small packet of papers.

Ms. Ellen said, "These papers are important. They are relevant to your mother's life insurance, pension, and 401K."

When Ms. Ellen had gone, Paige decided to wait and go through the papers tomorrow. Supper and a long soak in a warm tub sounded like what she needed now.

The next morning, Paige was sitting on the front porch, with a cup of coffee, watching the sunrise. She realized that death could come for anyone at any time, but being prepared to take care of the ones we love is our greatest gift.

"My mother is gone," Paige thought. "But she would never want me to give up. I am who I am, and have what I have because of her. Every day of my life is a gift. How many times did my mother tell me that? She was my most precious gift. I didn't have her long enough, and she was like no other."

Paige went back to the kitchen table and started going through the things that Ms. Ellen had brought yesterday.

The packet of papers contained another life insurance policy. It was for twenty thousand dollars, and Paige was the beneficiary. She was also entitled to fifty percent of her mother's pension. The 401K had a balance of fifty thousand dollars. It was in a trust that Paige could access at age forty.

The first box contained her mother's nursing books that she had collected and used for years. The second box held pictures, some covering Paige's life from childhood right up until the present, a picture of Christina's parents, and several awards and certificates for outstanding service at the hospital.

When Paige opened the third box, she wept. It was a collection of cards and letters from parents of the children her mother had taken care of while they were in the hospital.

"Strangers gave my mother more attention and credit than I ever did," Paige said. "It breaks my heart, but I will honor her by reading them all, if it takes me a year."

She took the boxes to her mother's closet so that everything would be in the same place. How humbling the things she didn't know about her mother had been.

Now, back to the envelope from the safety deposit box. When she got to the kitchen table, there was something on the floor.

"It's a feather. It must have fallen out of my mom's things. She must have been the one setting me up. I solved that mystery. Gotcha, Mom!"

The phone rang. It was a friend inviting her to lunch. She accepted, knowing she could open the envelope when she got back. Lunch turned into a shopping spree for the rest of the day. It was almost dark when she got home and once again the envelope would wait until later.

Chapter Thirteen

The next morning, Paige realized that she had to go back to work that night. She was ready and needed a distraction.

Sitting down at the kitchen table, she opened the envelope and found a one page, hand written note in her mother's flowing script.

Hoping and praying that this wasn't some kind of bad news, Paige was almost apprehensive to read it. It can't be simple if she hid it. If it was important, why didn't her mother just tell her?

"All your questions would be answered if you read it, dummy," Paige said to herself.

"Dear Paige, Search for Ankepi. I found him during the darkest time of my life. You can find him at the Angel Wall. He will tell you the story I couldn't. I make no excuses, nor do I have any regrets.

"Understanding will come, with time. I'm not so sure about forgiveness. Our relationship as mother and daughter may be shattered. Allow yourself to imagine how you would have reacted.

"Love you, I always have and always will. Forgive me, if you can. Search for the person who has the answers. I chose not to. I Love You, Mom."

Paige sat there speechless. "What the hell is this about?" She wondered. "I'm sure there might be things in my Mom's past that she didn't want me to know, but this I don't understand at all!"

She put the letter back in the envelope and left it on the table. It would take some time to figure this one out. For now, she prepared herself to go to work.

While she was getting dressed, the letter preyed on

her mind. Who was Ankepi? Why would her mom tell him things that she wouldn't tell her own daughter? She wasn't sure if she liked the sound of that!

When Paige reached work, Jay Jay was waiting for her at the nurses' desk.

"Welcome back," Jay Jay smiled. "It's going to be a busy night. We are a nurse short, and we've got five babies!"

"I'm ready, and I need the distraction." Paige laughed.

Paige helped Jay Jay with the babies. Then she cleaned the floors, and before she knew it, it was break time.

They went to break, and she told Jay Jay that her mom had prepared for everything. The house was paid for, and there was money in the bank. The one thing she wasn't prepared for was the drunk driver.

"Did my mom ever mention someone named Ankepi to you?" Paige asked.

"That's a strange name someone wouldn't forget, but I don't recall her ever mentioning it. Is there a problem?"

"I don't think there's a problem. It's just someone I want to talk to," Paige said with a puzzled expression.

Jay Jay whispered, "Let me know when you solve the mystery! But for now we'd better get back to work."

The rest of their night was busy. Paige didn't get a chance to visit the Angel Wall, and she was almost glad. She felt the painful memories of her mom would be more vivid there.

She decided to put this Ankepi person out of her mind. If he found her mom, he could find her, too.

For the next few weeks, Paige barely had time for a

break. There were at least seven babies every night and something always seemed to be left undone.

Jay Jay was going on vacation the following week, and Paige was dreading it because she wasn't close with the other nurses. She knew her job and wasn't worried, it was just more fun with Jay Jay there.

Chapter Fourteen

This had been a difficult week for Paige.

"It's going to be a good night tonight," Paige said with a smile. "Not one baby in the nursery, and no would-be moms in labor, for now. I'll enjoy this while I can."

She cleaned everything up and replenished all the bins by lunchtime. One of the nurses told her to take a good long lunch. They would call her if they needed her.

Paige went to the nurses' lounge, got a cup of coffee and decided to visit the Angel Wall. She couldn't help but laugh, since it was raining with some thunder and lightning, thinking this would be a perfect night for a ghostly encounter.

As usual, no one else was there. She sat on the bench close to the window and watched the lightning show. As the lightning became more intense, she turned her face from the window. Sadness and loss filled her heart, and all she could think about was her mom.

Someone was speaking, but she could barely hear them.

"Not funny," she said. "You're not going to scare me. I am intrigued with storms, and I enjoy watching them."

She no sooner got the words out of her mouth than a silhouette appeared. It was a beam of light shaped like a pencil. Within a matter of seconds, it was gone. It was probably a reflection from a flash of lightning coming in the window.

Paige stood up and started down the hallway, when the silhouette suddenly appeared again. She ran all the way back to the nurses' station.

When she got back, she realized that the same

person leaving the feather on the floor was setting her up. She now knew it wasn't her mother, or Jay Jay.

She chuckled and said, "I'll be ready for them next time!"

When she got off work that morning, she found herself consumed with thoughts of revenge. With two days off, she intended to have a game plan by the time she came back to work. They'd better be ready!

She got home and walked up to the front door and there was mere stillness. She thought, "A house brings things with it. I've got to remember the special ones."

Paige scarcely slept that day. Her world had been turned upside down, and her mother's final moments echoed over and over in her mind. "Maybe it's just my day for dealing with my emotional crisis," she thought.

It wasn't so surprising that she struggled so much at home. It had always been the two of them there, and this was the only place they called home.

Paige was sitting on the couch reading the newspaper, when she began entertaining the idea of going to nursing school. This would be a big step in getting on with her life, and a decision that would have made her mother proud.

Maybe this was simply a way to comfort her troubled mind. Maybe not! She had the money for school, and she had come to enjoy working at the hospital.

Thoughts of her mother that she couldn't seem to get out of her mind took her to her mother's room. She decided to get the cardboard box out of the closet, hoping memories of her childhood would ease her mind.

She set the box down on the floor, and sat down beside it. That way she could spread everything out and get a good look.

She pulled out her old report cards. For the most part, she always made A's and B's. Conduct was a different story! She loved to talk, she always seemed to get caught, and it had kept her in trouble.

Coloring books and drawings from the first grade through the fifth. Let there be no doubt, she would never become an artist. A stick man was about the best she could draw, but she did manage to color inside the lines.

She pulled out a small shoebox full of pictures. She laughed at her hair styles back then. Even funnier were the pictures of her toothless!

There were several dolls and two teddy bears that she remembered as her best friends. There was another envelope in the bottom of the box. She couldn't help but think, not again! The writing on the envelope read, important papers.

When she opened it, she found her birth certificate, hospital records, and a certificate with her foot print on it. Tears filled her eyes as she thought, this is where my life began. She read the birth certificate, and there was only her mother's name, no father's name.

She wasn't surprised because she knew that she had been adopted. Maybe one day, she would search for that answer, but it had never seemed important before.

The hospital records intrigued her! They showed her date of birth, her sex, her length and weight, but there was no hospital bill or baby picture.

"Mom must have adopted me soon as I was born," Paige thought. Because Christina's name was on the discharge papers twenty-four hours later.

I am so thankful, that my mom wanted a child to love and raise on her own. Most thankful, that she chose me.

Years ago Christina had told Paige that growing up as an only child was lonely. At the age of nineteen, she found out that she couldn't have children, and she was devastated.

There were very few men in Christina's life. None that absolutely took her breath away, or that she would want to spend the rest of her life with. A child was a different story.

Something of her very own to love and cherish, and bring a joy to her life that had been missing for so many years.

Paige closed her eyes, bowed her head and whispered, "I could've asked for no greater life, or love than you gave me. I was so blessed to have you in my life. I will always be grateful for you, the greatest gift God ever gave me."

Paige felt a sense of peace. Maybe this was a step in dealing with her mother's death. Being thankful for the years she did have, and all Christina brought to her life.

She put everything back in the box and put it back in the closet. "Enough for today," she said.

She had a smile on her face as she closed the door to her mother's room.

She whispered, "So many times I came to your room with a problem, and you fixed it. Today was no different. Thanks, Mom!"

Paige cleaned up the house and went to the grocery store. She knew that she had to go on with her life. There would always be grieving, but there also needed to be time for living.

She went to bed that night thinking seriously about going to nursing school. She was also thinking about ways to catch the person that was trying to set her up at work.

She came up with an idea. She would go to the Angel Wall every night on her lunch break, taking her IPad with her to capture any image or sound in the area. She was ready!

Chapter Fifteen

Paige pulled on to the hospital parking lot and there was Jay Jay.

"Wait up," she said. "I want to hear about your vacation."

Jay Jay replied, "I cleaned my house, visited my sister and didn't do much else. Did you make it okay without me last week?"

Paige laughed as she responded, "Someone tried to set me up at the Angel Wall. It almost scared me, but I've come up with a great plan, and the last laugh will be mine!"

When they got off the elevator, all they could hear was the sound of crying babies. They looked at one another and Paige said, "Welcome back!"

As they passed the viewing window of the nursery, Jay Jay counted the number of babies. She held up five fingers and said, "No easing into my first night back."

By break time the babies still hadn't settled down. Two were sleeping, and the other three were still crying. This was going to be a really long night!

Lunchtime came, and Paige went to the Angel Wall. She set facing the hallway hoping to catch whoever was trying to scare her.

Within a minute, she was aware of someone's presence. Was it real, or just her prankster?

Something was coming toward her, moving silently and effortlessly. The closer it came, the more splendid and impressive it appeared. As it reached her, the light around it was more vivid than the moonlight. It was almost angelic.

Then with a swirling gesture, it vanished.

That moment felt almost like a dream. Could it have been?

Paige stood up and took a deep breath. All she could do was breathe! This was no joke, she told herself.

"Let me get the hell out of here!"

She ran all the way back to the nursery.

Paige saw Jay Jay coming out of the nurses' lounge. She grabbed her by the arm and said, "You're not going to believe this!"

"Save it," Jay Jay replied. "We've got company."

There were two doctors in the nursery with a newborn. It was very sick and would be constantly supervised throughout the night.

Paige needed to find a place to sit alone and think things out. She could find no logic or reason for what had happened to her at the Angel Wall.

The longer she thought about it, the more she felt that telling Jay Jay might not be such a good idea. She didn't want her friend to think that she was crazy, but Jay Jay did tell Paige there had been stories about happenings at the Angel Wall.

"I'm convinced," Paige said. "There is something, or someone watching over the Angel Wall, but what does that have to do with me?"

The last four nights of her work week, Paige avoided the Angel Wall. It was inevitable that she would go again, and the thought of it gave her goosebumps!

When she got off work that morning, she stopped by Ms. Ellen's office to inquire about going to nursing school. Ms. Ellen hugged her neck, handed her a packet of paperwork and said, "Your mom would be proud of you, and so am I. Best of luck."

Paige felt good about her decision. The nursing

school was just across the street from the hospital, and the next semester started in three months.

Was she committed enough to go to school for four years and spend twenty- five thousand dollars? Was she doing this for herself, or her mom? These questions would need answers before she made any decisions.

She was so tired when she got to bed that she fell right to sleep. It wasn't long before she began to dream.

Chapter Sixteen

In the dream, Paige found herself standing at the Angel Wall with her mother. Christina's hand was stretched out toward the light, and she was whispering. Paige couldn't see anyone, but she didn't move any closer. Her mother's voice quivered as Paige heard her say, "It's in your hands now, Ankepi."

Paige sat up abruptly in bed, wide awake. Shaking and sweating, trying to catch her breath, she thought, "Was that real?"

First the letter and now the dream. That was the second time the name, Ankepi had come up. Paige dismissed it a few days ago, but there had to be more to this now.

"This scares the hell out of me!" Paige thought, deeply worried.

Finally, she drifted back to sleep, and it was late afternoon when she woke up. Feeling as if she hadn't been to bed all day, she said, "What the heck," and got up.

As if dealing with her grief wasn't enough, now she was dreaming about her mother and things that made no sense. She was losing her patience, quickly.

Strange things were happening. There was something that she was missing in all of this. Finding this Ankepi person couldn't come soon enough.

Paige wondered, could Ankepi be a ghost, or a spirit?

"Have I lost my mind?" She asked. "It seems like an odd question, but something is happening at the Angel Wall."

Her desire to find Ankepi had increased. It intrigued her because he was so elusive. There was something about

Ankepi that stirred the imagination.

Even though it was her night off, Paige was determined to go back to the Angel Wall, hoping to find some answers.

When she got to the hospital, she used the stairway instead of the elevators. Hoping to get to the Angel Wall unseen because there was no way to explain why she was there.

She got to the Angel Wall and couldn't help thinking, what if nothing happens? To be honest, she wasn't sure anything would.

There could be a hundred explanations for the things that had been happening. Her grief, the fact that she wasn't sleeping very well, and she had seen something she couldn't explain or prove was real.

"If this is a prank," Paige thought, "it's a damn good one!"

Something moved in the darkness. Paige tried not to appear nervous, but she felt herself quiver. Her heartbeat pounded faster and faster as it moved toward her. She inhaled and exhaled several times to slow her breathing and pounding heart down.

She didn't move the whole time, but she kept her eyes on it. If this was a ghost, coming face to face with it both terrified and fascinated her!

It stopped about five feet from her. Suddenly, it became a vertical stream of light. As it turned, it began to take on a form. It looked like wings were unfolding from both sides.

"Feathers!" Paige exclaimed. "This can't be. The feathers I found have been hints."

Looking at this creature was like looking at a beautiful painting. Glorious shades of light, and wings of brilliant white feathers. Its face had no definition of nose or mouth. Its eyes looked like two glass marbles reflecting a million colors from the light that surrounded it.

Then it spoke, "My name is Ankepi."

He looked into her eyes and called her by name.

"Paige, there is a story about your life. A story that was kept a secret even to the closest of those that knew your mother. I know who you are. I know everything."

Paige covered her mouth to hide the trembling of her lips. She stared at him, unmoving, with her eyes wide open. Then she closed her eyes and whispered, "Why are you here?"

Ankepi seemed to be considering how to approach this story. One thing was quite certain. Tonight, Paige's life would be changed, forever.

"I have been here for more years than you have been alive. My job is to watch over the children, and to give peace to anyone who searches for it at the Angel Wall," Ankepi told her. "Years ago, your mother found me, and told me an incredible story, but little did she know that I already knew it. She was desperate for peace, but unwilling to compromise to get it. It's time you know the truth."

Before Paige lost her nerve, she asked, "What does this have to do with me, if it's something that my mom did years ago?"

Chapter Seventeen

"Twenty years ago, March came in with a snow storm. The snow came down in big shimmery clumps. It was beautiful to look at, but within hours its depth had suspended everything.

"Your mother was here at work. Because of the snow, no one else could get to work, nor could those here get home. So your mom stayed. It would be hours before any of the other nurses could get here. If they could get here at all.

"A few hours later, the snow stopped. Christina walked outside to enjoy the beautiful snowfall. It was at least two feet deep on the ground, and there was so much snow on the tree limbs that they were bent the ground. The air was crisp and clean, but very cold."

Impatiently, Paige remarked, "Is this really important for me to know? Just give me the highlights, please!"

"May I continue?" Ankepi asked.

Paige gave a gesture with her hand as if to say, go ahead!

"Your mother turned around to go back in the hospital, when suddenly she heard a cry for help. She looked every direction, but couldn't see anyone. Then in the distance, she saw flashing lights on a car. Someone was signaling for help.

"She started trudging through the deep snow toward the car. She was moving very slowly trying not to fall. Her legs were freezing because her pants legs were wet. The snow was knee deep.

"When she finally got to the car, she opened the door, and a woman cried out that she was in labor, begging

Christina for help."

Paige's eyebrows went up and she said, "Many people help deliver babies. Just tell me the important parts. Can you please get on with the story!"

Ankepi's echoing voice commanded, "Listen! Your mother told her that she was a nurse and would help her, but there wasn't time to get her in the hospital.
The woman was young. Your mother could see that she was scared. She told her to lie down in the front seat, and push when she told her to.

"Shortly thereafter, the young woman gave birth to a baby girl.

"Your mother kept a pair of scissors in her pants pocket. At that moment she was glad she did. She cut the umbilical cord, took off her jacket and wrapped the baby in it. She told the mother that she needed to get the baby inside, and make sure she was ok. She would call security to come and help her.

"The woman began to cry. Christina asked if there was someone she could call for her, someone who needed to know that she and her baby were okay. But the young woman shook her head. There was no one.

"Christina's heart was breaking. This girl was all alone, and her family probably didn't know she was pregnant. She knew she had to get the baby inside. She promised to send help back for the mother, or at least, return herself.

"It was freezing cold outside. Christina held the baby tight against her chest, hoping her body heat would help keep the baby warm. It was a slow process taking one step at a time in the deep snow, but she made her way back to the hospital and took the baby to the nursery.

"She quickly cleaned her up, wrapped her in a

blanket, and laid her in a crib.

"When she called security, there was no answer. The baby was safe, so Christina grabbed a blanket and went back downstairs to get the mother.

"When she got outside the hospital doors, the car was gone! She didn't know what to think. Maybe she got herself around to the emergency room and got help.

"Christina went back to the nursery. Standing over the crib looking at the child caused your mother to wonder if leaving this child had been hard for the young woman. Maybe it was her only choice. Maybe she would come back."

As Paige listened, she tried to understand. Ankepi began to tell her more and more, every word burning a place in her mind.

"Watching this child stirred emotions in the deepest part of your mother's heart. She picked the baby up and held her close. Blonde hair and big blue eyes, in her opinion, the perfect child.

"She thought for a moment, realizing that she could take this child, and give her a good loving home. The thought of her becoming a ward of the state, in your mother's opinion, wasn't even an option.

"The consequences behind that type of decision would be great, but at that moment, only the mother and Christina knew about the child. It had become apparent that the mother didn't want this child and would probably never be seen again. One would be in as much trouble as the other."

Paige closed her eyes briefly, as in pain. She was swept up by her emotions.

"Go on," she said softly, completely absorbed in Ankepi's story.

"The phone rang at the nurses' station. It was one of the other nurses telling Christina that she was on her way. The snow plows were clearing the roads and traffic was beginning to move.

"Christina hung up the phone, and prayed for God to help her and forgive her.

"She took the child from the crib and wrapped her in blankets. She filled a bag with formula, diapers and other essentials for the baby. Fetching a laundry bin from the nursery, she put the baby and all the things in the bin and started down the hall to the elevator.

"When she got downstairs, she trudged through the snow, and took the baby to her car. She laid the baby in the front seat and cranked the engine to keep the baby warm.

"Back to the lobby, she emptied the bin, took everything to her car and put it in the trunk. She checked on the baby, and she was still asleep.

"She hurried back to the lobby, got the laundry bin and went back to the nursery. Then she waited on the other nurses to get there.

"Her heart was pounding, and fear took control of her mind. Was her life of loneliness the madness that drove her to do this? She was risking it all! But by then, of course, there was no turning back."

Chapter Eighteen

Paige let a moment of silence go by.

"Tell me, please tell me that child wasn't me!" She cried inconsolably.

Ankepi didn't answer.

"Why," was all she could say. Betrayal was what she felt.

"This delicate subject will not come without risk." Ankepi said. "It's for the best and long overdue.

"Within an hour, two nurses showed up. Christina gave them an update and left. She hurried to her car hoping the child was ok and not crying. When she got to there, the baby was asleep.

"The drive home was slow because of the snow covered roads. She began to weep, doubting her decision.

"As she pulled into the garage, she closed the door behind her, realizing that a life of looking over her shoulders had just begun. Not counting all the lies she would have to tell and remember.

"She took the baby inside. There was no baby bed, so she took a drawer from her dresser, emptied it and made a bed for the baby. As she laid the baby in the drawer, she opened her eyes and smiled.

"How could my mother let this happen?" Paige demanded.

Ankepi continued to tell the story, All Paige felt was betrayal. These events passed before her eyes like scenes from a movie.

"Your mother realized that she had two days off. She needed to get creative to explain this child. Her decision opened a whole range of problems that are not easily resolved. However, she made the choice. By then, of course, there was no turning back.

"Your mother had always talked about adopting a child. That would be her answer, one that she felt wouldn't be questioned.

"She would tell everyone that she kept it a secret, until it was final, fearing it might not happen. She knew she had access to all the necessary paperwork at the hospital. Pulling that part off would be easy. A phone call could get what she didn't have at work.

"Christina realized that this lie would be a part of her entire life."

Paige shook her head stubbornly, forcing her words out through clenched teeth. "My mom didn't give a damn about the truth. All she thought about was herself, and what she wanted!"

"I can imagine how frustrating all of this has been for you," Ankepi said. "You'll have to find a way to release this bitterness in order to move on."

Ankepi worried that no matter what he told Paige, she wouldn't be able to forgive her mother's actions.

Paige's voice grew intense, almost heated. When she spoke again, it was with anger. "This is too much to comprehend, too much to accept. I thought I knew her. I admired and loved her. Everything for twenty years was a lie! I need to know why, and it should've come from her, but that can never happen now. I feel betrayed, and I'm so terribly disappointed in the one person I trusted. All the values I hold dear are gone. What will I hold on to now?"

Chapter Nineteen

"I have revealed the secrets of Christina's heart." Ankepi said.

"Ankepi," she whispered. No response.

"Ankepi," she whispered again.

They were both silent. She held her breath and listened. No more words were spoken. He was gone.

The story was much more complex than she could have imagined. It didn't make sense, not for a moment. Overwhelmed, she didn't know what to do or how to act.

"I have to get out of here," Paige thought, running down the stairs and all the way to her car. She got in her car and just sat there in shock.

"What now?" she asked herself. "I guess I need to find out who I am."

She went straight home. When she got inside and closed the door, she screamed at the empty house, "It's all been a lie! Who the hell were you? Who the hell am I?"

In a few hours' time Paige's life, through no fault of her own, had turned into a tragedy once again. Her world was shattered. She had been lied to all of her life, and worse, she had accepted every word.

"Nothing could've been worse," was Paige's crushing comment. She was feeling hurt, and showing it. She would give anything to talk to Jay Jay, but that was out of the question. She didn't want anyone to know.

Paige went to her room and closed the door. Glancing in the mirror, she asked herself, "Who am I?"

She turned away from the mirror and answered herself honestly, "I don't know."

The tears in her eyes slowly ran down her face. It was hard to speak. She collapsed on the bed, crying until she fell asleep. But she awakened every hour on the hour as her mind tried to process truths that until tonight, she had never known existed.

Paige got up late that afternoon, needing to vent the frustrations that consumed her mind. After getting dressed, she drove to the cemetery. For once, she would do the talking. While she was driving, she couldn't help remembering a life of love and admiration for her mother. Even in death, her mother left her everything knowing that she would be taken care of.

When she got to the cemetery, her speech was all prepared, and she was going to give her mother hell! But as she walked to the grave site, cussing and yelling didn't seem appropriate. She would never get the answers she was looking for anyway.

She placed her hand on the headstone and stood there. Tears swelled in her eyes and somehow her thoughts of retaliation were gone. She knelt in front of the headstone, and ran her finger across all the words carved in it. At the end of a life there were so few words.

She whispered, "I can't think of any better life than I have had. One mother left me and another took me home. You freely gave all, while risking it all, at the same time. My real mother gave me life and nothing else.

"What would my life have been like without you? What you did will never change what we had. I only wish you had found the courage to tell me the truth, and I would've had the courage to listen."

Paige stood up, gazing down at her mother's grave.

"I will do the best I can," she cried. "My heart is broken, and my world has been shattered. I just need time. We'll talk again."

Paige felt like a fool. She got up and started walking

back to her car, knowing that an explanation would never be possible from her mother.

Something caught her eye. A young man was standing beside a grave with his head bowed. There were no flowers on the grave, or around it. He rubbed his cheek as if ashamed of his tears.

As she got closer, she asked, "Are you okay? I'm here visiting my mom's grave."

"I'm burying my father today." he replied. "A man I've only known for three months."

He raised his head up, looked her in her eyes and said, "I've seen you before at the hospital. I work there, too."

"My name is Paige," she said.

"I'm Nathan," he replied.

His story caught Paige off guard. He told her that three months before, he had received a phone call at work from a man claiming to be his father. The man had asked to meet him.

Nathan told her that when he was born, both of his parents left him at the hospital. He spent eighteen years in foster care and never was adopted.

When he met his father, for the first time, it broke his heart. The man was in ragged clothes, dirty and hungry.

He had told Nathan that he had moved from place to place since the day Nathan was born. Most times he lived under bridges, or any place that he could get out of the weather.

"How did you find me?" Nathan asked.

"I've always known where you were. I have a friend in this town who has kept me informed. I haven't seen your mother in years, nor do I know where she is."

"Why now?" Nathan had asked. "Why are you

contacting me now?"

His father had told him that he was dying. He was HIV positive from years of drug use, and he wanted to see his son before he died.

Questions weren't necessary any longer. It was too late for the answers to matter. Whatever he had done to Nathen, he did a hundred times worse to himself.

"My father told me his name was Guy. When he left, he promised to have a friend call me when his time began to run out. And he asked me to forgive him. As he began to walk away, he turned and said, 'You have shown me more kindness in fifteen minutes then I showed you in your lifetime. You are an incredible man.' I didn't know whether to stop him, or to knock him down, so I let him walk away. A decision I would regret the rest of my life."

Paige couldn't help but be fascinated by this man's story.

"I never saw him again," Nathan remarked. "Two days ago, I got a call that he had died."

"I'm so sorry," Paige said.

As she walked away, she turned briefly and said, "See you at work sometime."

He looked toward her and replied, "That would be nice."

After listening to his story, her situation seemed less earth shattering. His grief was unfathomable and like her, he was alone, too.

Her life was full of love, though the circumstances were unexplainable and heartbreaking. He had no one. Not even the hope that it would ever change.

Chapter Twenty

On the drive home, Paige thought more about his grief than her own. She understood his bitterness, but both of them were powerless to change anything.

"What would he think if he heard my story?" Paige wondered.

Both their parents left consequences that these two would live with for the rest of their lives. Acceptance would be hard, but inevitable. How they chose to deal with it would be up to them. There was no perfect answer.

"Maybe it's easier to know who you're not, than who you are." she said.

For now, she would keep her mother's secret. It would do no good to ruin everything she had worked to become all her life. She made a mistake, a big one, but there was no denying that she had loved her daughter.

Paige was looking forward to going back to work. She enjoyed her job, and was hoping to see Nathan again.

Her first night back was a doozie! Eight babies in the nursery. Jay Jay told her to clean and restock the bins. They had the babies covered.

When it was almost break time, as Paige was finishing the floors, she found a feather. She knew it was Ankepi's calling card, but she decided to stay away from the Angel Wall until she had her thoughts straightened out.

Then she remembered that Ankepi could be found anywhere.

The next two nights only got worse. Paige cleaned up more pee-pee, poo-poo and puke from eight babies than she could've ever imagined.

She was taking her lunch break in the nurses' lounge when in walked Nathan. One of the nurses stood up and said, "Come on in Dr. Bass, and have a cup of coffee."

Paige almost choked on her sip of coffee. She hadn't realized that he was a doctor.

"How's everything going tonight, Paige?" he asked.

Paige laughed and said, "Really busy with eight babies!"

He sat down beside Paige and she couldn't help but smile.

"I'm sorry," he said. "I didn't mean to overwhelm you with my story at the cemetery."

"I've got a story as sad as yours. Next time, I'll tell you mine." Paige said as she shook her head.

They chatted for a few moments, and Paige realized that she found the young doctor easy to talk to. All too soon, he stood up.

"Gotta go. I've got two patients waiting to be transferred from emergency to regular rooms. Let's do breakfast one morning."

"Love to. Just let me know when you have time." Paige replied smiling from ear to ear.

Becoming friends was a diversion they both needed. If nothing else, when she did tell him her story, she felt he would understand.

When he had gone, Jay Jay stuck her head in the door and grinned, "Good looking, young, and a doctor, too! You're going to have to tell me about this!"

Paige stood up, did the happy dance, and replied, "I just met him, but believe it or not, we have something in common, sorta."

The rest of the week didn't get any better. There were still eight babies in the nursery. Their last night at work there was only one baby in the nursery, so everybody caught up on their breaks while looking forward to their week-end off.

Paige decided to visit the Angel Wall, almost positive she would find Ankepi there. When she turned to go down the hall, she felt a light breeze around her. There was no avoiding the moment.

"What do you want from me?" she asked.

"To know what's in your heart," a calm voice said from the shadows.

"Stop!" she demanded. "It's still in a million pieces. There's nothing but pain."

"Silence will not heal your wounds," Ankepi told her. "Nor will these scars heal overnight."

She sat down and turned her face away.

"Please go!"

Ankepi stood there, staring at her. He shook his head then turned away.

She looked straight through him. Then she began to cry. With tears on her cheeks she muttered, "When I close my eyes, I can see her. Her clothes, the scent of her perfume, and her smile that always fixed everything."

"Put the heartaches and disappointments behind you. Don't overthink the situation, don't dwell on the negatives. Everybody goes through their share of losses. There will always be set backs, but you can overcome them," Ankepi told her.

She listened, straining to hear his words.

Ankepi whispered, "It does get easier with time."

"Does it?" she asked, not believing it was possible.

There was a moment of silence, and Ankepi was gone.

Time allowed Paige to search for an answer. Maybe not the one she was hoping for, but one she could live with. Either way, she had to go on with her life.

Two days off, she thought. No more sitting at home, hiding as if I did something wrong. No one knows, or has to know, until I'm ready to tell them. If I ever do!

Suddenly, Paige stopped, surprised. "Oh! I sound just like my mother!"

At that moment, she realized how she had judged her mother, for a decision to keep the truth hidden, and she was going to do the same thing.

How quickly the memory of calling her mother a liar came back to her.

"The apple didn't fall far from the tree." she said to herself.

She sat down on the couch in shock, thinking what a hypocrite she had become.

"Can I live the truth?" she asked herself.

Paige opened the drawer of the coffee table beside her and pulled out a tablet and pencil. "I'll write everything down, good or bad, about my mom, and see where it takes me."

The List of Good and Bad

My mom was born to two loving parents that gave her a wonderful life.

I was born to a mother who abandoned me, and a second mother that chose to steal me.

My mom was an only child, so was I, I think.

My mom grew up having great love for children. She went to nursing school and joined the neo-natal team, so that she could work with children.

I've come to enjoy working with children as well. I plan to go to nursing school and follow that same path.

At the age of nineteen, a physical required for nursing school, revealed that my mom couldn't have children.

Very shortly, I will undergo that same physical, but my hope is that I can have children someday.

After my mother finished nursing school, her parents were killed in a train wreck. They had nothing to leave her, so she worked her way through school.

Two months ago, I lost the only mother I had ever known to a drunk driver. My mother took care of everything by saving and paying things off, so I won't have to struggle for anything.

My mom died with deep dark secrets in her heart. If you practice a lie long enough, it becomes real. I don't believe she lied to protect herself, she lied to protect me.

As time went on her lie was accepted. The only person that could've caused her any problems was my birth mother. She lied, too, but it was to protect herself, not me. Not once, then or now, has she ever come forward.

"The sky didn't fall," Paige thought, after making her list. "I'm still okay."

What was the bond that held mother and daughter together? The short answer was love. The more Paige thought about it, the clearer she saw things.

She felt a sudden ray of hope. She forced a smile and said, "Enough, I've had enough, for today. I'm tired of thinking."

Her mother's story complicated her life. Dealing with it and living with it left her few choices. Even though she knew the truth now, what would it take to accept it and move on?

"Day by day," she thought. A hot bath and a good night's sleep seemed the perfect combination to wind down the day.

Chapter Twenty-One

Sleep came easier that night. The acceptance of her own inability to change anything was finally setting in.

The morning had passed Paige by when she finally woke up. It was almost lunchtime. She felt rested and ready for a good day.

The phone rang. It was Nathan. "I got your number from work, and would love to take you to lunch if you're available."

"Sounds good to me," Paige replied. "I can meet you in about an hour. Where would you like to meet?"

He told her about a small restaurant downtown. Nothing fancy, and they wouldn't be bothered by co-workers.

She agreed and hung up the phone. She really wanted to be friends with Nathan and hoped they could share their stories. It would surely bring a much needed peace to both of them.

When she got to the restaurant, Nathan was waiting for her. It was a small place that seated about thirty people, but it had an outside patio area. Perfect for a private lunch.

Nathan pulled out her chair for her and said, "I'm glad you could make it."

"Quite the gentleman," Paige said with a smile. "I wouldn't have missed it!"

They ordered lunch and after several minutes of talk about work, their lunch was served. Once they had finished eating, Paige felt compelled to share her story.

At times, Nathan shook his head in disbelief, and then he nodded as if he understood. Somehow, as they talked, a peace captured them both, and they seemed at ease.

"It's been quite an afternoon, hasn't it?" Paige asked, as she made an effort to smile.

"I've learned that the most painful part of growing up is discovering that nobody's perfect. Not even your parents," Nathan remarked.

Paige whispered, "Don't you agree, though, there's a difference in being perfect and honest?"

"Oh yes!" Nathan said. "But what difference could it make now? Our lives are what they are, and we are who we are."

Paige discovered that listening to Nathan's story had changed her feelings about many things.

"This has been fun!" She said with a grin.

Nathan laughed out loud and remarked, "Thank you, for taking my mind off of so many of my own depressing thoughts."

"Thank you, for lunch and some very inspiring conversation. I need to get home, though, duty calls tonight."

Nathan stood up, pulled out Paige's chair and replied, "I really enjoyed our time together today. I hope we can do it again sometime."

They said their good-byes as they walked to their cars. It was apparent by the look on their faces that they both had enjoyed their afternoon together.

Paige was so relieved that she had told Nathan her story. Saying the words seemed to ease her pain. She realized that what began as a desperate choice by her mother, turned out to be the best choice for her life.

When Paige got home, she went straight to her mother's room. She walked in the room and just stood there. Suddenly, everything changed.

After a few minutes, she knelt down beside the bed

and whispered, "You have and always will be my mother. Though our choices may have been different, I thank you for giving me a chance at life, and I will always love you as my mother. I learned that I was capable of rage because rage is brief, but hate. No, it endures. I forgive you, and for now your secret will remain deep within my heart."

She felt an endless love, and loss at the same time. It wasn't easy to express her feelings, but somehow, she felt empowered.

Before she lost her nerve, she looked at her mother's picture beside the bed and whispered, "Telling the truth could do more harm than good." She bit her lip to hold back the tears.

She got ready for work, and thoughts of her lunch with Nathan brightened her spirit. When she backed her car down the driveway, she stopped for a moment to gaze at the brilliant, full moon and the pattern of the stars. Lights that would shine forever in the darkness.

Chapter Twenty-Two

The nursery was in total chaos when Paige got there. There were five babies in the nursery and three mothers in labor! The cleanup person hadn't been there for two days. Paige was way behind.

Jay Jay was in overdrive, barking orders and shaking her head.

"No rest for the weary tonight," she said. "Do all you can, while you can because there won't be time to sit on the can!"

By break time, Paige had the floors cleaned and most of the bins restocked.

"Let's get a quick cup of coffee," Jay Jay said. "We could have three more babies at any time!"

Paige gave her a thumbs up sign and replied, "Got lots to tell you when we get time."

By lunchtime there were seven babies in the nursery.

"All hands on deck," Jay Jay yelled out!

For the rest of their shift, there was a baby in everyone's arm almost constantly. Lunch break was out of the question!

Paige had hoped to see Nathan, but more than that, she wanted to go to the Angel Wall and find Ankepi. She had a lot to tell him.

The next three nights were unchanged in the nursery, but by her last night at work, all the babies except two would be gone home.

When she got to work that last night, there were only two babies in the nursery. She was ready for the slowdown. If at all possible, her trip to the Angel Wall would happen tonight, and maybe Nathan would come by for a visit, as well.

As if life wasn't cruel enough on its own. Paige realized that she had wreaked havoc on herself out of anger and stupidity. It gained her absolutely nothing, and it was past time to let it go.

When she finally got to the Angel Wall, she set down on the bench, turning her head from side to side to watch for Ankepi.

She set there for a few minutes and nothing happened.

"Why do you hide yourself, Ankepi?" She asked.

There was no answer.

Paige lowered her head. Before she lost her nerve she whispered to Ankepi through her tears, "I want to talk. I have searched my heart."

For a moment, there was silence on both sides. The lights began to blink, and when they stopped, Ankepi was right beside her. The thought of it made her tremble. She watched him, completely absorbed.

Ankepi took her by surprise. He asked, "What do you want from me?"

She looked into his eyes and said with a sobbing voice, "I need to thank you. I can live with my mother's decision. I know that in time the scars will heal. She saved my life and that's all that matters. It's the only life I've known, and I'm grateful."

"There were many secrets in your mother's heart. This was just one," Ankepi said as he rose up.

"I don't ever want to know any more of them. Let her rest in peace. It doesn't matter!" Paige cried. "All I could see was the embarrassment of her choices instead of her sacrifice. I doubt her love for me no more!"

Ankepi paused. His words and the knowledge that they were fact, frightened her. She tried to not let fear show in her eyes, but intrigued, she took it all in! She didn't blink or budge, but simply listened, straining to hear his words.

"Very well then," he said. "You shall carry your mother's secrets deep within your own heart. You will always wonder why, but when the time comes, and it will, we'll talk again."

"The reality of it is, I loved my mom. I believe in what I'm doing-even if it's the wrong thing. Even after what she's done, I forgive her," Paige said.

Ankepi turned and faced her. He whispered. "I will always watch over you, as I always have."

Then he vanished.

"We all suffer in our own way." Paige thought. "There is value in dealing with death, and also value in moving beyond it.'

Paige went back to work, feeling good about her decision of forgiveness and the courage to try to move on. It was all quiet in the nursery, so she got caught up on her work.

In a couple of hours she would start her two days off and hopefully hear from Nathan. Something she missed during her busy week.

Someone was calling her name. It was Jay Jay, and she said, "Let's get together this week-end, and you can tell me the good stuff about you and Dr. Bass!"

Paige replied, "Looking forward to it, unless I get a better offer!"

"Won't hurt my feelings. I'll just wait a little longer for the juicy details, but it better be good!" Jay Jay said with a smile. "Go home, I'll call you later."

Paige took the elevator to the lobby. When she stepped out, she was almost face to face with Nathan. They walked and talked, heading toward the front door.

"I would love to take you to lunch on Sunday if you don't have any other plans," Nathan said.

Paige responded with a smile and said, "Sounds great! I actually have another story to tell you. This one is really going to be unbelievable!"

By this time they were standing outside the hospital front doors. Paige pointed her finger and said, "There's someone standing at my car. It looks like a woman."

"Let's watch her for a minute, and if she doesn't move on, I'll walk you to your car," Nathan whispered.

They stepped aside to let a man in a wheelchair through the front door, and when they looked back toward Paige's car, the person was gone.

About that time, Nathan's pager went off, and he said, "Duty calls. I'll call you later!"

When Paige got to her car, there was something under her windshield wiper blade. It looked like a note.

She pulled it out and opened it.

It read, "Christina did a wonderful job of raising you. All your life I have watched you from a distance, but that's all I could do. I'm sorry. Maybe now!"

Paige turned her face from side to side looking to see if anyone was around.

"Oh, God!" She screamed. "Could that woman that was standing beside my car have been my mother?"

She held the note close to her chest. Her heart was racing and tears filled her eyes.

"Could it be?" She wondered.

Bio

Born and raised in Mississippi, Margaret Eubanks still resides there today with her adopted dog, Frank.

She is the author of four books, available in paperback and on Kindle –

Whispers

Good Night, Sippi, I Love You

Ankepi: The Keeper of the Angel Wall

The Tattered Bag: A Life Remembered.

Made in the USA
San Bernardino, CA
07 September 2013